TANGLE
and the
SILVER BIRD

FOR ERICA, JILL & SOHIER

BENEDICT BLATHWAYT

Copyright © 1989 Benedict Blathwayt
All rights reserved
First published in Great Britain 1989 by
Julia MacRae Books
A division of Walker Books Ltd
87 Vauxhall Walk,
London SE11 5HJ

Blathwayt, Benedict
   Tangle and the silver bird.
   I. Title
   823'.914 [J]   PZ7
   ISBN 0-86203-319-5

Printed in Singapore by
Tien Wah Press (Pte.) Ltd.

Julia MacRae Books

A division of Walker Books

The little people of the Northwoods lay dozing in the hot afternoon sun. All except Tangle, who sat by himself. What a dull way to spend the day, he thought.

It was still and quiet; there was no sign of an adventure. Tangle was very bored.

And then he heard something. Was it the growl of distant thunder? The buzzing of a swarm of bees? It grew nearer and nearer, louder and louder…

Tangle sprang to his feet. Whatever could it be?

Suddenly the sky overhead filled with a
deafening roar. A huge silver bird flew low over
the tree tops. The Northwoodsmen scrambled
down their burrows in panic.

"What is it?" they asked each other, trembling.
"What does it want?"
"Where did it go?"

Burr put his head above ground and saw Tangle.
"Quick!" he called, "come below!"

"I'm not afraid," said Tangle. "The silver bird has
flown towards the lake, let's go and see it."

"I'm coming," said Burr, but he didn't feel
very brave.

Tangle and Burr ran to the lake and there, close to the shore, floated the silver bird.

"Look at that!" whispered Tangle. "Did you ever see such a monster? I think it's asleep. I'm going to take a closer look."

"I shouldn't," said a friendly goose.

But Tangle and Burr took no notice. They climbed aboard the enormous bird. How cold and hard its skin felt beneath their feet.

"I don't like it," said Burr.

Even as he spoke, the silver bird woke up, and began to move. Across the lake it skimmed, faster, faster…

"Hang on!" shouted Tangle.

And suddenly they were in the air. Up, up, flew the silver bird. Their home woods grew further and further away. It was like a dream. Tangle shut his eyes.

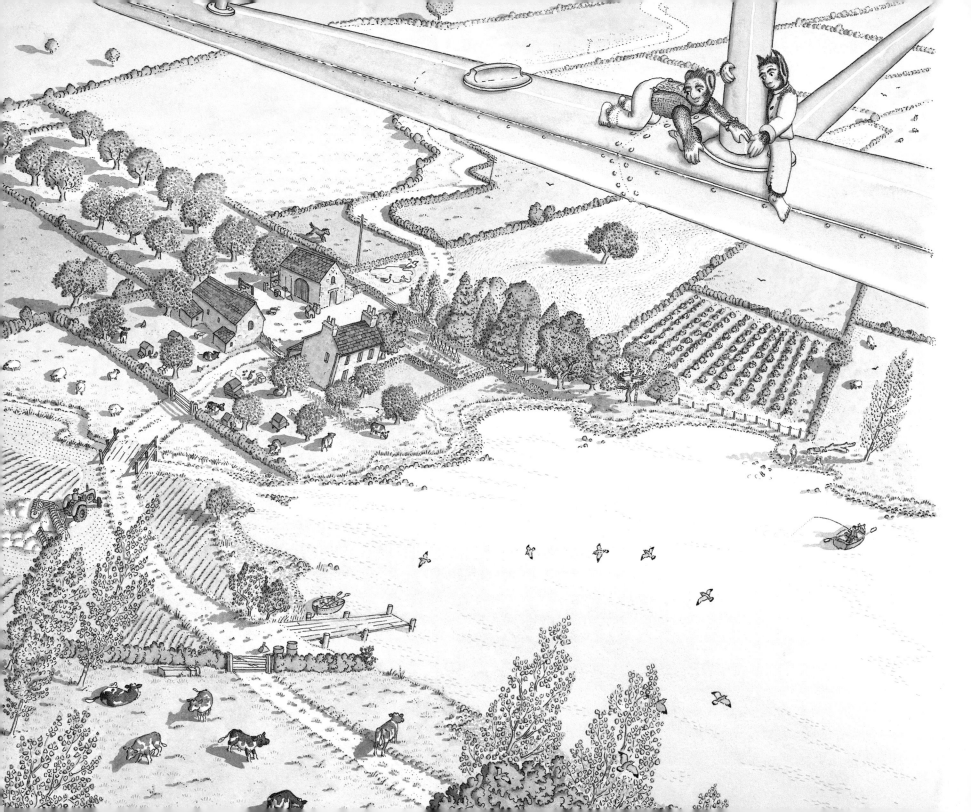

Tangle and Burr held on tightly. When Tangle dared open his eyes again he saw a new world far below. The silver bird dipped its nose and the lake came rushing up to meet them.

"The bird is going to land," cried Tangle.

As the silver bird touched down in a shower of spray, Tangle and Burr were thrown head-over-heels into the water. They swam for the shore.

"Hurry up," called Tangle. "I'm freezing. Let's go and explore."

Where was this strange place? And what were these frightening creatures?

"Come on," said Tangle, "we must find somewhere safe to rest."

They climbed as high as they could. A mysterious country lay all around them.

"I'm hungry," said Burr, when they woke early next morning.

But none of the creatures they met seemed willing to share.

The other animals had plenty to eat, but Tangle and Burr didn't like any of the strange new tastes.

"Look," said Tangle, "there's something going on up there." So the two friends climbed through an open window and into a room full of good things to eat.

What wonderful food. What a great feast!
Tangle and Burr ate their fill, never noticing
the dark shape creeping stealthily towards them.

And then the creature SPRANG.

Tangle and Burr ran this way and that with a clattering and a crashing and a crunching, the creature hard on their heels.

Such a chase! Such a dreadful mess! And then for a moment they seemed safe.

"Keep going," squealed Tangle. "It will soon be after us again."

Burr dived into a chicken coop and hid himself amongst the chicks. But Tangle missed him and ran straight past, into a hen house. The hens scolded him as he tried to hide in their straw.

And there he was found. A huge hand picked him up, put him in a basket and carried him away. Help, thought Tangle, what will happen to me, and where is Burr?

The hand put Tangle down in a large room,
full of the most marvellous and puzzling things.
He began to enjoy himself.

"Oh, I *do* wish Burr could be here!" sighed Tangle.

The gentle hands picked Tangle up again and set him down on a high wooden platform. Suddenly, he felt like a prisoner. Escape seemed hopeless, and even if he reached the ground – what then? There were unfriendly eyes below, watching his every move, and waiting…waiting.

But help was at hand next morning.

"Burr!" cried Tangle joyfully, "I thought I'd never see you again."

"Come on, sleepy-head," whispered Burr, "there's danger everywhere, and no time to talk. My friend the hen has a plan to help us escape."

As soon as they had climbed down from the tree,
there was a pounding of paws close behind them.
"Quick," yelled Burr, "follow me!"

At the very moment Burr and Tangle squeezed through a tiny hole at the back of the chicken coop, the clever hen pulled the door prop away.

Their enemy was trapped inside!

"There's no time to lose," called Tangle, as Burr waved goodbye to the hen.

But when they got to the lake the silver bird refused to wake up. "Oh, please hurry," begged Tangle, "you *must* take us home!" They stamped and shouted, but it was no good: the enormous bird floated silent and lifeless, ignoring their cries.

"I warned you about that silver bird," said a
voice. "Now I'll help you get home safely."
It was the friendly goose.

"Hop on and hang on," said the goose.

The journey seemed to take forever,
but at last they saw their very own
woods below them.

"What an adventure," said Burr. "Will anyone ever believe our story?"
"No," said Tangle, "I don't suppose they will."